The Girls Of Lakeview Academy

Trust Casefiles, Volume 3

Lee Cushing

Published by Lee Cushing, 2016.

This is a work of fiction. Similarities to real people, places, or events are entirely coincidental.

THE GIRLS OF LAKEVIEW ACADEMY

First edition. August 27, 2016.

Copyright © 2016 Lee Cushing.

ISBN: 979-8201047054

Written by Lee Cushing.

Chapter One

Her clothes torn and bloodied, Daphne McBride saw the red haired woman standing ahead of her amidst the trees.

Crouching like a wild animal as she moved through the undergrowth towards Catherine Jordan, she launched herself forward as soon as she was close enough.

Smashing Catherine to the ground, Daphne snarled, her fingers grasping a large rock nearby. Raising the rock above Catherine's head, she smashed it down, leaving a deep gash on the side of Catherine's face.

Continuing to slam the rock down several times, Daphne only stopped the assault when she heard Catherine's skull crack, blood streaming from the mess of flesh that used to be Catherine's face.

Dropping the blood covered rock onto the ground, Daphne glanced at the Adlet and other women coming into view. She gave out a primitive snarl to warn them to stay away from her kill.

Leaning down over Catherine's unmoving form, she torn into the flesh with her teeth, tearing it away from Catherine's throat with hungry intent.

Daphne screamed as she woke and sat upright, sweat dripping from her dark skin.

The light from the opposite side of the bed came on.

"Another bad dream?"

The soothing American accent made her glance at Catherine lying next to her, "I just want them to stop." She paused, looking at her lover for a few moments. "They're worse when you're not here."

Catherine sat upright, smiling as she kissed Daphne's bare shoulder. "Nathan said it might help if you talk about it."

There was a long pause before Daphne replied, "I was eating you."

A gentle smile appeared on Catherine's face, her hand moving up Daphne's thigh. "Doesn't sound so bad so far."

"Not like that." Daphne did begin to smile for a brief moment which faded as she continued, "I mean really eating you, tearing you apart, everything." She bit her lower lip, "And I was liking it."

Running her fingers through Daphne's black hair, Catherine focused on her face. "Everything that happened on the island is in the past." She fell silent for a moment, checking the time on the digital clock on Daphne's side of the bed. "Hang on a minute."

Watching Catherine leave the bed and vanish from the room, Daphne waited for several minutes for her to return.

Something clenched within her closed fist when she came back, Catherine settled back on the bed and revealed a small velvet lined box, offering it to Daphne. "I was going to save this for later, but happy Valentine's Day."

Taking it from Catherine's outstretched fingers, she opened it and stared at the diamond ring inside, her focus shifting to Catherine's face. "It's beautiful."

Catherine caressed Daphne's cheek, "Not as much as you are." She smiled, "Try it on."

Slipping the ring onto her fingers, she looked at Catherine again, unable to stop a faint smile appearing on her lips. "Thank you."

Leaning forward, Catherine kissed her on the lips for a few moments before switching off the bedside lamp. "Now let's get back to that talk about eating me, the fun kind."

The smile widening into a broad grin, Daphne disappeared under the duvet and Catherine lay back, her head resting on the pillow as her girlfriend got to work.

Chapter Two

"No, Mum." The woman with lemony coloured hair in the van continued talking on her mobile phone, "I haven't got time for another blind date for a few days, I'm out on assignment." Victoria Fisher paused, watching the lorry pull into the yard at the side of the mortuary. "I have to go."

Disconnecting the call, she opened the door to the van and stepped down, pausing to remove the Beretta from the dashboard.

Starting to move closer, she saw the light come on through one of the rear windows of the building and came to a sudden stop under an overhead street lamp.

She watched the rear door to the mortuary open and a rather overweight man step out and approach the truck.

Jumping down from inside the truck, a sandy haired woman approached the man and made a quick movement with her wrist, slashing open the man's plump neck.

She was about to start back for the van when she saw the man shaped shadow overlapping with her own.

Barely having time to see the decayed features of the man behind her, Victoria felt the rotting hands on her throat the moment before her head was twisted to one side.

Leaning against the wooden fence overlooking the crocodile shaped boats below, Daphne continued to look down at the water as Catherine approached from the cotton candy booth.

She rested her arms on the post, "Ever hear of a place called Barton Grange?"

Daphne turned towards her girlfriend, "I think it's somewhere in Lancashire. Why?"

Folding her arms, Catherine exchanged glances with her lover. "Alex wants me and Cutter to take a trip there, the area co-ordinator asked for help in locating a missing operative."

Disappointment appeared on Daphne's face, "What about what we had planned for tonight?"

Catherine gave her a soft smile and leaned forward to kiss her, "I've convinced Cutter that we should delay leaving for a few more hours and I've spoken to Mario at the restaurant, he's agreed to let us have a table provided we can be there in half an hour." She kissed Daphne again, "But the last course is going to have to wait until I get back."

Sitting in the back of the limousine, the plump blonde teenager watched as the car started along the road towards the large castle like building on the other side.

Glancing through the side window at the lake on one side of the road, Myriam Perrin heard the French accent of the elegantly dressed brunette sitting next to her.

"Smarten yourself up, young lady. Your father wants you to make a good impression on your first day."

Giving the woman a quick look, Myriam's fingers obediently fumbled to fasten the school blazer she was wearing.

"And no more getting into fights. Your father will not be happy if he has to send me all the way back here again."

Myriam answered with her own soft French accent, "Yes, Miss Monet."

Climbing out of her side when the limousine came to a halt, Miss Monet stepped on the gravel and looked at the driver. "Bring in Miss Perrin's bags."

Approaching the large oak door, Miss Monet was about to press the buzzer when it opened.

Emerging from inside, the red head barely reached beyond Miss Monet's shoulders. Ignoring the woman towering over her, Jessica Chapman walked straight towards the teenager. "You must be Miss Perrin. If you will come this way."

Miss Monet started to move towards the open door.

Blocking her, Jessica shook her head. "I'm sorry, but we only allow students and staff beyond this point without an appointment. For security reasons, I'm sure you understand."

Miss Monet seemed ready to explode with anger, but simply turned to watch the driver removing several suitcases from the back of the limousine. "What about her bags?"

"Wait here and I'll send someone out to collect them." She turned her attention back to Myriam, "Please follow me."

Stepping through into the entrance hall with a flight of stairs along the side wall, Myriam glanced at the two portraits hanging just under the balcony above the opposite wall.

Jessica noted her interest, "That's Mr Barton and Miss Simpson, the founders of the school before it was relocated to England. It was Mr Barton's family that established the local salt mining industry and founded the town which was given his family name." She caught sight of the expression that had formed on Myriam's face, "I'm boring you, aren't I?"

The girl politely shook her head.

Glancing back towards the still open door with Miss Monet waiting on the other side, she turned back towards Myriam. "Can you give me a minute?"

She watched Jessica walk through an archway into a long corridor leading away from the main hall.

Returning after two or three minutes, Jessica was followed by a scruffy haired man in overalls. The janitor heading outside, she stopped when she reached Myriam. "Come on, I'll show you to your room."

Glimpsing the janitor collecting her bags from where the limousine driver had placed them, Myriam started to follow Jessica up the stairs.

Hearing the tone of the front door bell, Daphne closed the book she was reading and made for the hall.

Opening the door to the flat, she gave the dark goatee bearded man a smile when she saw him leaning against the metal railing overlooking the playground below. "Want to come in?"

Following her inside, Forrest King entered the lounge and collapsed onto a long couch, noticing the ring on her finger as she sat opposite him. "Cat suggested I drop in."

"There's no need, I'm fine." Daphne looked at him, "But I am glad you're here." She hesitated before continuing, "Cat isn't here as much as I'd like her to be. What with the new shelter due to open in London and almost constantly out on assignment for Alexandra, then there's the full moon when we have to be locked up."

Forrest edged himself forward, "Catherine loves you. That ring, Cat gave it to you, didn't she?"

Nodding, Daphne stretched out her fingers to show it off. "Last night."

There was a pause before Forrest continued, "Kate gave her that ring, it means the world to Cat and she gave it to you. What does that tell you?"

Standing up, Daphne walked to the fireplace, resting her hand on the mantle as she glanced back. "Can I ask you advice on something?"

Rising from the couch, Forrest approached her. "Go ahead."

Daphne bit her lower lip, "I was thinking about asking Catherine if she minds if I move back in with her. I know I made a big thing about maintaining my independence before we started seeing other, but everything's different now. I don't want to be without her."

Forrest gave her a long look and his smile widened, "She'll say yes in a heartbeat if you ask her, quicker even."

There was a trace of doubt lingering in her voice when she answered, "Sure?"

He took her hand and let her see the ring on her finger, "Without a doubt."

Walking through the opening into the amusement park lit by a multitude of overhead lamps, the brown haired man with the ponytail stopped, waiting for the youthful looking blonde to reach him.

Taking a deep breath to savour the cold night air, he turned his attention towards one of the arcades nearby, speaking with a East European accent. "I believe we go this way." Walking through the opening into the arcade, he approached the nearest booth, glancing at the woman inside. "Contact Co-Ordinator Glinyeu, inform her that I require to speak with her."

"I'm sorry, but I don't..."

The man interrupted her, "Give her the message." He pointed to the entrance to the Goldmine ride, "My assistant and I will be waiting over there."

Chapter Three

Slipping on her coat to leave for the night, the dark red haired woman collected her cane from the side of the office desk and began limping towards the exit.

Stepping into the outer office, she passed the dark skinned woman talking on the phone, speaking with her New Orleans accent. "Goodnight, Miss Goodman."

Vicki clicked her fingers, motioning Alexandra Glinyeu to stop her departure. Continuing to talk on the phone for a few more moments, she hung up and glanced across the desk. "There's a guy waiting by the goldmine ride who insists on talking with you."

"Okay, I'll take care of it."

Watching Alexandra begin to leave again, Vicki grabbed the Double Eagle from the top drawer of her desk, "Need back up, Ma'am?"

Alexandra stopped and shook her head, "I don't think that will be necessary."

Continuing into the passage, she made her way to the stairs leading up to the amusement park. Stopping briefly by the door at the top, she pulled it open and emerged into a half packed cafe.

Not given a second glance by the customers as she headed outside, Alexandra followed the lit path until the fake mountain exterior of the goldmine ride came into view.

Watching her coming down the long concrete walkway, Vladek stepped forward as she reached him. "My name is Anton Vladek." He glanced back at the girl with him, "This is Katarina, she assists me."

"What exactly do you wish to speak with me about?"

Vladek waited for several teenage couples to start up the walkway, "There have been concerns about a number of your recent decisions. In particular, the recruitment of Agents King and Jordan to our organisation. Their reputation prior to joining us is questionable to say the least. And there is the decision that led to the loss of Major Braxton."

"I stand by my choice concerning Mr King and Miss Jordan, they have proven themselves to be exceptional field operatives." Alexandra paused before continuing, "And about Major Braxton, you're not the one who had to inform her family that she would never be coming home."

Catching sight of more people walking past them, Vladek again waited until they were out of earshot. "Perhaps we should continue this review in the privacy of your office."

"We'll need the proper clearance."

Vladek glanced at Katarina when she finally revealed her Russian accent, "Like she says, we will need full and unrestricted access to this facility."

Getting out of the red van, Catherine stepped down onto the concrete.

Walking to the other side of the van, she approached the closed door of the late night convenience store.

Glancing back as a forty something man with a marine style haircut jumped down from the passenger seat, she pushed her way into the store.

Walking straight to the counter, Catherine took a quick look round to make sure there were no customers. "Alexandra Glinyeu sent us." She cast her thumb towards the man who followed her inside, "That's Cutter, I'm Catherine."

The teenager pointed to the door next to a cardboard display holding a small collection of cheap DVDs, "Michael's in the back."

"Thank you." Catherine followed Cutter into a storeroom full of boxes.

The dark haired man sitting behind a metal desk looked up, "Miss Jordan, Mr Smith?"

Catherine sat on a worn wooden stool, "Tell us about your missing agent?"

"Her name's Victoria Fisher." Michael swung round on his chair to face them, reaching back to remove a folder from his desk. "Over the last few weeks, there have been a number of thefts at mortuaries throughout the region and the only things taken were bodies. I sent Victoria to keep surveillance on one of the possible targets three days ago."

"But the premises weren't hit until last night?"

Michael nodded when he heard Cutter's Texas accent. "Nearly a dozen bodies were taken."

Getting up from the stool, Catherine moved to the wall and leaned against it. "I'd like to take a look at any reports your agent made."

"That could be a problem." Replacing the folder on his desk, Michael swung back on his chair to look at her. "Victoria preferred keeping her reports at her flat."

Catherine straightened up, "Give us her address, we'll go and collect them ourselves."

Leaving the school dining hall, Myriam reached the stairs leading up to the dorm rooms.

Glancing back as a group of other girls in uniform passed her, she started up to the top. Turning into the passage, she walked towards the door to her assigned room.

Turning the handle, she pushed the door open. "Excuse me."

The softly spoken French accent made the long haired redhead stop looking through one of Myriam's bags, a strong Australian accent coming from her lips as she turned, "Sorry, bad habit." Walking past Myriam to the door, the girl pushed it shut.

"Who are you?"

Returning to where she had been previously standing, the redhead opened one of the windows, letting it a strong draught of cold air. "It's Laura." She flashed Myriam a quick smile, "Laura Graham."

"I'm Myriam Perrin."

Moving to her side of the room, Laura reached into the pocket of the school blazer dumped on her bed. Removing a pack of cigarettes, she returned to the window as she slipped one out. Preparing to light it, she glanced back at Myriam. "Want one? There's plenty spare."

Myriam silently shook her head.

"Don't worry about getting caught, the worst they do is send us to the headmistress and she'll come down harder on me than you."

Stepping towards the vacant bed, Myriam collapsed on the mattress, watching Laura take another puff on the cigarette between her fingers. "You've been in trouble before?"

"Hardly." Laura remained by the window, "She's my Mum."

Picking the lock to the door of the flat, Catherine pushed it open and stepped straight into the lounge.

Turning on the light, she approached the small glass table in front of the couch and began checking the magazines laid out on the surface.

Cutter closed the door and proceeded to a bookcase, glancing at a framed picture of Victoria and her mother as he passed.

Slipping out a journal from under the magazines, Catherine tossed it to Cutter. "Take a look through that for anything useful, I'm going to take a pee."

Ignoring her going towards the bathroom, Cutter started to look through the journal, his gaze focusing on the various entries.

His concentration was broken when the front door opened.

Victoria smiled when she saw him, "I missed you." Moving towards him before he could speak, she gripped each side of his head and kissed him.

He felt the coldness of her skin when her lips touched his.

"Do you two want to be alone?"

Her head snapping round towards Catherine, the pleasant expression on her face fading in an instant.

Seeing the picture of her and her mother, Catherine turned her gaze back to Victoria. "Miss Fisher, your co-ordinator has been worried about you."

"Cat, she's stone cold."

Cutter's words made Catherine start to move forward. "Why don't you come with us, Miss Fisher?"

Victoria lashed out, her hands reaching for Catherine's throat.

Grabbing both of Victoria's wrists, Catherine twisted Victoria over the couch, her head smashing into the glass table.

Seeing the shard of glass protruding from Victoria's forehead as she got back to her feet, Catherine was ready when she charged.

Managing to twist her way behind Victoria, she was able to grapple Victoria to the carpet, a sound of desperation in her voice as she turned her head towards Cutter. "Get something to restrain her."

Watching him rush out through the front door of the flat, Catherine slammed her knee into Victoria's back, pressing down hard to stop her from squirming free.

Returning after a few minutes with a coil of rope, Cutter unravelled it and began to bind Victoria's wrists together.

Grabbing the rope restraining her, Catherine pulled her up onto her feet and started pushing her towards the open front door.

Leading the way outside, Cutter reached the open doors at the rear of the van.

Victoria made an attempt to run when she got close enough to the van doors.

Maintaining her grip on the rope binding Victoria's wrists together, Catherine slammed her knees against the back of the van, using the momentum to push Victoria into the van.

Shoving her further inside, Catherine and Cutter banged the doors shut.

Moving to the passenger side, Cutter opened the door and climbed onto the seat, glancing back to make sure Victoria was still lying on the metal floor. He waited until Catherine was settled behind the wheel, "I'm not sure about the local containment facilities."

Catherine started the engine, "So we take her back to Durden's Bay, I can keep her subdued for three hours or so."

Chapter Four

Punching her fist down on the pillow, Myriam looked across at Laura's bed, the constant pig like snoring keeping her awake.

The digital alarm clock next to the bed revealed that it was only a few minutes passed midnight, she slithered out from under the warm duvet. Her bare feet sinking into the thick carpet, she moved towards the window.

Reaching for the latch, she glanced back at Laura, wondering if a blast of outside air would wake her enough to quieten the snoring.

She pushed the window open.

Beginning to turn away, Myriam caught a glimpse of something and looked back.

A group of girls in their uniforms were running towards the line of trees close to the road.

Watching them disappear from sight, she heard the snoring from Laura's bed go silent.

"It's bloody freezing." Laura began to focus her eyes on Myriam. "Close the window and go back to bed."

"But." Myriam returned to look out at the row of trees with no longer any sign of the girls. Pulling the window shut, she looked at Laura settling back under the covers.

Driving along the road running alongside the wall of the amusement park, Catherine turned the corner and started down the slope. Bringing the van to a halt by the security station in front of the closed gate, she waited until the guard on duty cleared her and Cutter. The metal gate rising, she drove under as soon as it was high enough and parked in the first available space.

Getting out of her side, Catherine walked to the back of the van, waiting for Cutter to come into view.

Catherine pulled open the rear doors and focused on the still bound woman, "Come on, don't make harder than it needs to be."

Victoria remained perfectly still.

Waiting a few moments for a response, Cutter climbed inside and crouched over her. Pushing her over onto her back, he looked back towards Catherine. "She's dead, really dead this time."

"We still better put her in containment just to be safe. Then there's the report."

Jumping down, Cutter grabbed Victoria's feet and began pulling across the metal floor on the van. "I can take care of the paperwork."

Catherine flashed him a quick smile, "Thanks. It'll be a nice surprise for when Daph wakes up in the morning."

Taking a look at his watch, Cutter tapped on the display. "Morning?"

The comment made her smile, "It's not morning until after I've been to sleep." Catherine waited until he had removed Victoria's body and closed the van doors. "I'll see you later."

Turning onto the driveway leading to the large house, Alexandra drove along the gravel and parked her Toyota in front of the closed garage door.

Stepping out, she removed her cane from next to the seat and pushed the car door shut. Supporting herself as she approached the front door of the house, she stopped when she heard the crunching of footsteps on the gravel behind her.

"There is still much for us to discuss."

Alexandra turned to face Vladek, "Can't this wait until morning?"

He watched Katarina move behind her, "I'm afraid not, the matters we must discuss are of the most grave importance."

Doing her best to remain silent as she unlocked the door to the flat, Catherine typed in the code to stop the burglar alarm from going off.

Gently pushing the door shut, she approached the door to Daphne's bedroom and turned the knob slowly.

Removing her jacket as she stepped inside, Catherine's gaze focused on Daphne asleep in the bed and she began to take off the rest of her clothes.

Approaching the empty side of the bed, she slipped under the duvet and turned to face her girlfriend.

Catherine placed her head on the pillow and closed her eyes, slipping her arm over her lover's waist.

Turning over in the bed, Daphne lips curled into a smile when she opened her eyes. "Nice try."

"Sometimes I hate that you're such a light sleeper." Catherine moved her to Daphne's shoulder and pulled her close enough to kiss, "I wanted to surprise you in the morning."

Daphne propped herself up on her elbow, her other hand moving to caress Catherine's cheek. "Did you find that missing agent?"

"I'm afraid she was dead." Catherine looked across at her girlfriend, "She was still walking around, but she didn't seem like any of the other things I've come across. We subdued, restrained and brought her back here for some answers. But by the time we got back, she was really dead."

Daphne watched Catherine settle onto her back and moved to snuggle up against her, "Her body could have been possessed by a Vetala."

Letting Daphne rest her arm over her breasts, Catherine looked at her. "So what do these Vetala do?"

She felt Catherine's knee moving up her inner thigh, "They possess dead people and cause trouble mainly." A smile appeared on her face, the feel of Catherine's fingers reaching down between her legs. "They're attracted to..." She stopped long enough to let out a soft moan, "People in power."

Repositioning herself until she was looking down at the face her heart was beating for, Catherine lowered her head and let her tongue run over her girlfriend's nipples. Her head moving up until she was face to face with Daphne, she lowered her lips towards Daphne's mouth.

Waiting until the kiss that Catherine initiated ended and their lips parted, Daphne threw her head back on the pillow.

Kissing Daphne's breasts in turn, Catherine started working her way down her lover's body with a mixture of kisses and soft gentle licks of her tongue.

Watching the masked pathologist complete his autopsy of Victoria's body, Cutter saw him look out through the glass and shake his head.

Heading away from the medical section, he started up the steps further along the passage. Turning right at the top, he continued until he reached the door to his office.

Entering, he removed his current journal from a bookshelf on the wall and settled behind his desk.

He picked up a pen and opened the journal to begin writing in it. About to start, he stopped when the phone on the side of his desk began to ring.

Picking it up, he began to smile. "Yes, Vicki, I'm still here. I was just about to start on the report." He paused for a moment, "Okay, I'll be right up."

Leaving his office, Cutter hurried up the next flight of stairs and along the passage. Reaching the door to the operations centre, he ignored the people working at various desks and approached the one that Vicki was standing next to.

She nodded when he came to a stop, "A police report from Barton Grange came in a few minutes, a number of bodies have been found. It appears that they were among the bodies taken during one of the thefts."

Cutter glanced at the redhead sat in front of the desk, "Vera, are there any CCTV cameras in the vicinity of where the bodies were found?"

"Give me a minute." Vera Corbett worked on the desktop for a few moments, "There's no footage of the location where the bodies were found, but I can bring up something from a few nearby cameras."

"Start four hours before the bodies were discovered."

Vera acknowledged Cutter's instructions, "I'll put it up on the big screen."

Turning their attention to the screen on the wall opposite the door, Vicki and Cutter watched several images appear stacked side by side.

"Speed it up." Cutter moved closer to the screen, studying the images for a few minutes. "There on five."

Vera responded by pausing the image on the fifth screen.

"Take it back about thirty seconds."

Moving to his side, Vicki saw a pair of girls come back into view. "Zoom in on the uniform."

The emblem on the school blazer becoming clear, Cutter glanced back at Vera. "Can you identify the school these girls attend?"

Vera started the search. After a number of school uniform emblems appeared on her monitor, she looked up at Cutter. "Lakeview Academy."

"That's an interesting discovery."

Cutter turned immediately to look towards Vladek standing in the open doorway with Katarina right behind him. "Who are you?"

He stepped further inside the room, "I am Anton Vladek and I am your new co-ordinator."

Chapter Five

Parking her van next to a battered looking VW Beetle in the neighbouring space, Catherine climbed down and closed the door.

Approaching the car, she rested her arms on the roof, smiling as Daphne got out from the other side. "I still could have given you a lift."

Daphne walked round the front of her little car and slid her arms around Catherine's waist, leaning in to kiss her. "And if Alexandra sends you out on another assignment?" She took a step back, "Or maybe you might like a break and stay at your place?"

Reaching out, Catherine grasped the belt on Daphne's jeans and pulled her back. "My place is wherever you are." She returned the kiss she had been given a few moments ago, "I love you."

Taking Catherine's hand as they started for the entrance to the amusement park, Daphne glanced towards her. "I do want to ask you something?"

"Sure, go ahead." Catherine stopped and looked back when Daphne came to a halt, their fingers still locked together. "What is it?"

Daphne paused for a second, "What would you say if I asked if I could move back in with you?"

Placing her hands on each side of her lover's head, Catherine wasted no time in returning to her and released all her feelings in one long kiss, "Give me ten minutes and I'll have some guys ready to move all your stuff in." She continued to beam with delight, "I don't think I've said I love you enough today."

Slipping her fingers around Catherine's hand, she started walking alongside her. "It doesn't get old."

Still holding hands when they reached one of the amusement arcades, the two of them stopped.

"I suppose I better see if Alex wants me to do the follow up." Letting go of Daphne's hand, Catherine gave her another kiss. "I'll see you for lunch?"

"The usual place?"

Catherine nodded, "I love you." She smiled, "There, I said it again."

Leaning in for another kiss, Daphne briefly slipped her arms over her girlfriend's shoulder. "Well, I love you too." Pulling back, she began to walk away. Stopping after a few yards, she glanced back.

Catherine was still standing in the same spot.

Smiling, Daphne gave a little wave and turned away again.

Watching her disappear from sight, Catherine stepped into the amusement arcade. Giving a nod to the man in the change booth, she reached the staff only door and waited for the buzz of the lock being released.

Entering the short passage beyond, she reached the steps and started going down to the corridor below.

Making for one of the doors further along the wall, she opened it and entered. Not bothering to stop, she glanced at Vicki. "The Boss in?"

Pushing the door open before Vicki could say anything, Catherine came to a stop when she saw Vladek behind the desk.

"Where's Alex?"

He stood up and moved round the desk towards her, "It's Agent Jordan, isn't it? We haven't been formally introduced, I'm Anton Vladek."

Catherine stared at him, "I'll ask again, where's Alex?"

"Co-Ordinator Glinyeu is..." A smile appeared on his lips, "Otherwise engaged." He glanced at the personal belongings on Alexandra's desk, "I will be running this department until she returns." He returned behind the desk and sat down, "Concerning this operative, Victoria Fisher, that you and Agent Smith brought in last night." He looked across the desk at Catherine, "Agent Smith has uncovered fresh information that needs looking at I believe. I advise continuing your investigation and see what turns up."

She lingered for a moment before walking out to the outer office. Approaching Vicki's desk, she looked back towards the open door. "Do you know where Alex is?"

Vicki shook her head, "That's what concerns me. Miss Glinyeu never went anywhere without me arranging for a security detail to accompany her."

Catherine glanced back at the open door, "Keep an eye on whoever he is. And better let Forrest know what's going on, ask him to nip over to Alex's house and take a look round."

"What about you?"

Catherine started for the outer door, "I've going back to Barton Grange with Cutter, see if we can find out what happened to that operative."

Out of Vicki's line of sight, Vladek watched Catherine leave.

"So did you ask her yet?"

Daphne turned to face the blonde haired woman chewing on the end of her glasses, "Ask her what?"

Sarah Abrams propped herself up against the edge of Daphne's desk, "You're big moving in speech. You've been practicing it all week." She smiled at the look appearing on Daphne's face, "You think none of us round here noticed what you were doing?" She moved away from the desk, "So, did you ask Cat or not?"

Nodding, Daphne could not stop the ecstatic grin appearing on her face. "This morning, she said yes."

"You'll be expecting me to help out with moving your stuff to her place I suppose?"

Daphne shook her head, "Don't worry, Catherine's going to make all the arrangements, you're not going to have to lift a finger." She placed her hand on a large stack of folders, "At least not after you've taken these to processing."

"Right." Sarah slipped her fingers under the bottom folder and lifted them from the desk, "If I'm not back in twelve hours, send out a search party."

Carrying the thick stack to the door, Sarah stopped as Vladek opened it for her and let her pass into the corridor.

Vladek let the door swing shut and started towards Daphne, "I thought it would be prudent to introduce myself, Miss McBride."

The unfamiliar voice made her turn, "Mr Vladek I presume."

"Your friend has told you about me?"

Daphne watched him remove a journal from the nearest bookshelf, "Catherine's not my friend, she's my girlfriend. There's a difference."

"I'm sure there is, Miss McBride." He skimmed through several pages before replacing it on the shelf he took it from. "Tell me, how do you feel about your girlfriend condemning you to a life where you turn into a vicious, flesh eating monster once a month? Wouldn't it have been kinder to have left you on that island with no memory of who you were for the short time you had left?"

"Catherine did what she did because she loves me, she brought me back."

Vladek moved behind her desk, "Yes, she did." He turned back to face her, "You were still under the Adlet influence when she found you. It took an injection of her own blood to ensure you would change into a werewolf during the next full moon. A rash hope of a desperate lover. Fortunately for your girlfriend, she got lucky Your first transformation restored your mind."

She remained silent as he walked past her.

Vladek stopped by the door, "Since you've been back, has there ever been a moment when you've craved the taste of fresh human meat?"

"No." Daphne's answer was adamant.

He pulled the door open, "Living with this affliction can be a slippery slope, Miss McBride." Vladek turned back to look at her, "Be sure someone doesn't push you down it."

Chapter Six

Picking up the tray with her lunch from the dining hall counter, Myriam started walking between the tables of chatting girls.

Passing a dark haired girl with red and blue highlights appearing in strands overhanging her face, she reached the table where Laura and two other girls were sitting.

Walking to the other side of the table, Myriam sat into the chair, barely taking her eyes off the girl with the red and blue highlights. "She's one of the girls I saw sneaking out last night."

Turning her head, Laura glanced towards the table where the girl was sitting. "Oh, you're talking about Rachel and her friends."

"Who are they?"

Laura looked away from them, "Freaks and mean bitches. Always picking fights with anyone they don't like, which pretty much sums up every girl here who's not one of them." She gave the group another quick glance, "Probably best just to stay away from them all together."

Turning onto the driveway leading to Alexandra's house, Forrest parked his Porsche in the empty space outside the garage door.

Getting out, he rang the bell and waited for a few minutes. Eventually pulling out a lockpick from his pocket, he pushed it into the lock and began jiggling it about.

Turning the handle after unlocking the door, he pushed it open and his attention fell on the two smashed vases on the carpet.

He continued into the lounge, stepping past the broken television screen. Reaching down, he trailed his fingers across the solitary bloodstain on the carpet.

"It's not Co-Ordinator Glinyeu's if that's what you were thinking."

Forrest turned as he stood up, giving the newcomer a broad grin. "You must be this Anton Vladek I've been hearing about, Cat and Daph aren't exactly your biggest fans at the moment."

Moving behind the couch, Vladek placed his hands on the back. "I am not here to be popular, Agent King."

"Let's cut to the chase, Anton." The smile faded from Forrest's face, "Where the hell is Alex?"

"Co-Ordinator Glinyeu is..." Vladek met Forrest's gaze, "Indisposed for the moment. I've told all this to Agent Jordan."

Forrest started towards him, "I'm afraid that isn't going to be good enough, I insist on knowing where she is."

"I cannot give out that information." Vladek remained silent until Forrest was standing directly in front of him, "She is on a very sensitive assignment, details of which could prove to be dangerous for her if they became available to certain parties."

Looking back at the shattered television screen, Forrest stopped by the edge of the couch. "Nothing you've told me explains what happened here."

"What happened here doesn't concern you, Agent King, not at this time." Vladek walked through back into the hall, stopping by the front door. Opening it, he turned to watch Forrest coming out of the lounge behind him. "Any other questions you have are going to have to wait, there are matters that demand my immediate attention."

Stepping outside after Vladek opened the front door, Forrest glanced back at him. "If I find out you did something to Alex..."

Vladek cut him off, "You'll kill me. Believe me, Agent King, I've heard those kinds of threats many times before." Remaining by the open doorway, he watched Forrest get back inside his Porsche and begin driving away.

Waiting until the car turned onto the road at the bottom of the driveway, he closed the door and walked back to the kitchen.

Opening the door to the cellar, he descended the concrete steps and glanced at the woman with the pillow case over her head.

He looked at the iron manacles holding her wrists against the arms of the metal chair she was sitting in. "Shall we pick up where we left off?"

Giving out a scream when the skin on her wrists began to bubble from contact with the iron restraints, the unidentified woman gave up after a few moments.

Vladek selected an iron spike from the table next to the chair where she was being held and impaled the sharp point into her thigh.

Chapter Seven

Closing her textbook, Myriam slipped it into her bag and got up from behind the table. Stepping into the space between the rows of tables, she slipped into the line of girls leaving the classroom.

She came to a stop just on the other side of the door, letting the girls behind her continue filing out into the corridor.

Pulling out a folded piece of paper from the breast pocket of her school blazer, Myriam opened it out and glanced over her class schedule.

Keeping the paper open between her fingers, she started to move along the passage with the other girls. She stopped again when she saw the girl with the red and blue highlights by the door to the school gym.

Approaching her, Myriam gave a smile as Rachel Shaw turned to look at her. "Hi, I'm new here." She raised the paper in her hand, "Can you tell me where the room 14 is?"

Rachel made no attempt to speak and simply pointed to an adjacent passage.

Watching her start to walk away, Myriam moved after her. "I'm Myriam."

Coming to an abrupt stop, Rachel half turned. "I don't care."

"I saw you sneaking out last night."

The statement made Rachel complete her turn to face Myriam, "Forget what you saw, it's none of your business."

"I wasn't going to tell anyone." Myriam tried to stare down Rachel, "I thought we could be friends."

Rachel grabbed Myriam's blazer and shoved her back against the wall, a venomous tone creeping into her voice. "I don't want to be friends with a fat bitch like you, now go away and stay out of my business."

"You don't have to be mean."

Releasing her hold on Myriam's blazer, Rachel took a step back, a smile appearing on her face. "I like being mean."

Myriam started to turn and Rachel's arm suddenly blocked her from moving forward.

"Tell anyone about me and my friends leaving last night and I'll make your time here hell, is that crystal?"

Nodding in response to the threat, Myriam waited for Rachel to lower her arm, glancing back over her shoulder as she was allowed to walk away.

Gripping the wooden railing at the end of the pier, Forrest looked at the water below.

Hearing footsteps on the wooden planks behind him, he glanced back as Daphne stopped next to him. "I thought we should speak out here, less chance of Vladek showing up to surprise us." His gaze returned to the view of the ocean, "I checked out Alex's place. It looks like something bad happened there last night. Vladek was there as well."

"You think he did something to her?"

He lowered his head, "I honestly don't know, but I get the feeling he's dangerous. I definitely don't trust him or anything he says, reminds me of a politician."

There was a pause before Daphne spoke, "I think he threatened me."

Forrest's eyes shot towards her, "Are you sure?"

Shaking her head, Daphne looked out from the pier. "That's the problem, I don't know."

"Well, what did he say?"

Daphne turned her head towards him, "He was talking about what happened on the island and how Catherine managed to bring me back. Then he seemed to suggest it'll only take a nudge to make me start to like eating human flesh."

Putting his hands on her shoulders, Forrest gave her one of his wide grins. "Neither me or Cat will ever let that happen to you, that's a promise."

Fastening the pin striped jacket she was wearing, Catherine glanced from the backseat. Removing the glasses from the jacket pocket, she slipped them in front of her green eyes.

"How do I look?"

He glanced at her reflection in the mirror for a moment before turning his gaze back to the road ahead, "Like a lawyer."

"Exactly the look I was going for." Catherine finished fastening the tie she had put on, glancing forward as the limousine turned onto the road next to the lake.

Reaching for the handle as Cutter parked close to the school entrance, Catherine opened the door and stepped out onto the gravel.

She walked up to the door and rang the bell, glancing back at Cutter still behind the wheel.

Turning back when she heard the door open, she looked at Jessica standing on the other side. "I'm here to see Ms Graham."

"Miss Carter?"

Catherine nodded at the mention of the alias she was using, "That's right."

Stepping back to let Catherine enter the hall, Jessica closed the door behind her, turning towards a blonde haired girl coming down the stairs. "Karen, would you please escort Miss Carter to Ms Graham's office?"

Karen Jolanka glanced at Catherine, focusing on her face for a few seconds before she spoke. "Yes, Miss Chapman."

"There are things I have to do, Miss Carter." Jessica gave Catherine another glance, "But Karen will take care of you."

"Thank you." Catherine watched the girl start walking towards the archway, starting to follow her.

Following Karen into the passage on the other side of the archway, she ignored the girl glancing back at her.

Karen stopped by a oak door at the far end of the passage and knocked on the wood. Listening for permission, she turned the handle and pushed the door open. Taking a few steps inside, the girl watched the short haired redhead look up from behind her desk.

"There's a Miss Carter waiting to see you."

Angela Graham stood up and moved from behind the desk, "Thank you, Karen. Show her in."

Stepping back as she watched Catherine enter the office, she started to continue, stopping only when she heard Angela's voice.

"Please close the door before you go."

Karen turned and reached for the handle, giving the back of Catherine's head one last look before she closed the door.

She remained on the passage side of the door for a few seconds. Turning quickly, she began hurrying back the way she had come.

Almost breaking into a slow sprint by the time she passed through the archway back into the hall, Karen hurried up the stairs and along the corridor.

Stopping when she reached the door to one of the dorm rooms, she opened it and entered the room.

Karen pushed the door shut as Rachel and two of the other girls looked up at her, "There's a hunter here, she's talking with Ms Graham right now."

Chapter Eight

Following Angela back into the hall, Catherine came to a stop by the main door.

"Thank you for the tour, Ms Graham. I have been most impressed by the facilities you've shown me." She waited for Angela to open the door, "I'm sure you'll be hearing from Mr Collins concerning his daughter's enrolment after he's gone over my report."

Angela watched her start walking towards the parked limousine outside, "I'll be looking forward to hearing from him."

Opening the rear door, Catherine slipped onto the leather seat, an amused smile appearing on her lips as she pulled the door shut. "Home, James."

Cutter started the engine, "Very funny."

Driving alongside the lake, he turned off the road and onto a rising muddy trail leading behind the row of trees.

Waiting until the limousine halted by a parked red van, Catherine stepped out and approached the man sitting on a fold out chair. "Where's Forrest?"

Tasting the hot coffee from the plastic cup in his hand, the ginger haired man shook his head. "He isn't here." Ian Knight glanced at his watch before having another sip of his drink, "He didn't come, he said he wanted to see if he can find out more about our new boss." He looked up at her, "It is just standard surveillance?"

"Is there anything standard about this job?" Catherine turned at the sound of the side door opening, glimpsing a mattress laid out inside.

Stepping down from inside, a tall brunette closed the door, a steaming cup of coffee in her hand. "The kettle's still hot if you or Cutter want a cup."

"Thank you,"

Amanda Ward glanced back as Cutter closed the limousine door and made for the van, turning back towards Catherine after a brief moment. "How about you?"

Catherine shook her head, "I'm okay." She moved to collect one of the folded up chairs propped against the side of the van, "Why don't you two get a couple of hours rest or whatever you want to do, let me and Cutter take over for a while." She watched Ian and Amanda give eager nods, smiling as their fingers locked together.

She sat back and raised the binoculars to her eyes, her attention diverted to the playing field at the side of the school building as girls with hockey sticks began to emerge.

Missing the ball when it was smashed away from directly in front of her, Myriam caught sight of the glare that appeared on Rachel's face.

She remained still as the ball was slammed by Rachel's hockey stick into the net, her head turning slightly as she became aware of several girls lining up behind her.

Rachel and Karen stopped side by side in front of her.

Nowhere to go, Myriam watched the group move until they were surrounding her.

Taking a step forward, Rachel halted when she heard the whistle, turning her head briefly to see the gym mistress blowing it again. She looked back, directing her best intimidating voice towards Myriam. "Lucky girl. This time."

Watching the girls surrounding her start to follow Rachel as she left, Myriam waited until they had disappeared through one of the doors at the side of the school building.

She started to move towards the door that the other girls had entered, waiting a few more moments before opening the door.

Checking Rachel or her friends were not in view before committing herself to entering, she hurried along the passage until she came to the archway leading to the hall.

Hurrying up the stairs, Myriam continued until she reached the door to her dorm room. She rushed inside and closed the door behind her.

Approaching the desk of drawers on her side of the room, she opened it and pulled out one of the drawers inside.

Rummaging through her packed away clothes, she removed her mobile phone, glancing back as Laura entered the room.

"I saw your run in with Rachel and her friends, what did you do to piss those bitches off?"

Removing the phone from the drawer, Myriam turned away from the desk of drawers. "I wanted to be friends with her, she seemed like she might be fun."

Laura closed the door, "You know better now."

"Yes I do." Myriam tightened her hold on her phone, "And if they try sneaking out again, I'm going to make sure your mother knows all about it."

A smile appeared on Catherine's lips as she listened to Daphne's voice on the mobile raised to her ear.

"I love you too." She lowered the phone and turned it off, glancing back as Ian and Amanda emerged from the back of the van.

Glancing at the empty space where the limousine had been parked, Amanda walked up to the back of the chair. "Where's Cutter?"

"He went to pick up his van and return the limo." Catherine picked up the binoculars and took a look down at the school, "Personally, I think he wanted to have a go at picking up the blonde that we requisitioned the limo from."

"It is Cutter we're talking about. He's a professional, an ex seal." Amanda stopped when she saw the grin appear on Catherine's face, "You're having fun with me, aren't you?"

Catherine got up from the chair and handed the binoculars to her, "Just a little." She started towards the van, unzipping her thick jacket to reveal the shoulder holster underneath. "Wake me in four hours or if we get some activity down there, whatever comes first."

Sitting in the darkened room, Myriam kept her focus on the slightly ajar door.

Her drooping head jerking up when she heard low voices on the other side coming closer.

Moving from her bed, she collected her phone from the desk close to the window and started towards the door.

She reached the door, waiting until she heard the whispering girls pass. Taking the chance to peer through the crack, she saw Rachel carrying a gym bag towards Karen and two blonde girls who were waiting at the fire door by the far end of the passage.

Gingerly popping her head beyond the door, Myriam watched one of the girls ahead of Rachel pushing down the lever to open the thick door.

Letting all but Karen go first, Rachel stopped at her side. "I'll give you a ring when we're on our way back and you can let us back in."

Myriam ducked out of sight when Karen closed the fire door and returned to her dorm room.

Waiting until she heard Karen closing the door to her room, she stepped out into the passage.

Hurrying to the fire door, she pressed down on the lever and pushed the door open. She glanced back before stepping onto the metal fire escape and began rushing down.

Stopping when she reached the gravel floor surrounding the school, she peered round the side of the building just in time to glimpse the three girls disappearing into the woods.

Chapter Nine

"Cat, they're on the move."

Ian's voice waking her, Catherine rolled onto her side and reached for the handle.

Turning as the van door slid open, Amanda continued watching the girls hurrying away from the school through the binoculars. "What do you want us to do?"

Catherine stepped down onto the grass, snatching a spare set of binoculars from one of the chairs. Looking in the same direction as Amanda, she focused on the girls from the school.

Returning the binoculars to the chair, she rushed back to still open door of the van and grabbed the Ruger from her discarded shoulder holster lying close to the mattress. "Stay here and tell Cutter when he gets back I've gone after them."

Catherine set off running, stopping when she caught sight of the girls. Giving them a few moments to get further ahead of her, she moved along the edge of the hill, keeping the girls in view.

Coming out from the mass of trees, Rachel looked across the road at the warehouses visible through a wire fence.

Approaching the gate, Rachel removed the rusted and open padlock. She placed the gym bag on the ground and unzipped it, pulling out several silver bladed machetes. "Jenny, Susie. Just like last night."

The other girls taking one each, she pushed the gate open and entered first. Glancing around, she made a sudden dash for the large concrete pipes stacked together.

Seeking shelter inside the nearest pipe, she waved to the other girls who immediately ran to join her.

Rachel moved to the other end of the pipe when Jenny and Susie had joined her. Peering out towards one of the warehouses, she watched the door swinging back and forth in the winter breeze.

Motioning her friends to remain hidden in the pipe, she dashed for the warehouse door and looked inside at the truck wide entrance to the salt mine.

She began to back away after several minutes, figures starting to appear from the darkness of the salt mine.

Racing back to the concrete pipe, Rachel concealed herself with Susie and Jenny moments before the warehouse door was pushed open from the inside.

Watching from the cover of the pipe, she saw the first Vetala emerge from the warehouse, the light from the moon revealing the rotting flesh under the sparse clump of red hair.

Rachel moved back further inside the pipe, glancing towards her friends. Passing them, she hurried to the opposite end of the pipe.

Stopping before coming out the other side, she watched several of the Vetala start towards the open gate. Looking back at her friends, she nodded when no more came into view.

Waiting until the slow moving Vetala were almost at the gate, she ushered Jenny and Susie to follow her as she moved into the shadows.

She tightened her grip on the machete, moving towards the gate once the Vetala were out of sight.

Reaching the gate to continue following the possessed corpses, Rachel spun round when she heard one of her friends scream.

Rotting hands gripped Jenny's throat and twisted.

Rachel lashed out as her friend's body collapsed at the Vetala's feet. Swinging the machete out of anger, she sliced through the throat of the walking corpse.

The Vetala staggered back and collapsed close to where Jenny's body had fallen.

Grabbing Susie's arm, Rachel began pulling the shocked girl away from the other Vetala that were approaching.

Making a dash for the open gate, Rachel froze when she saw more Vetala blocking the route to the road.

Glancing back, she watched several of the Vetala pause by Jenny's corpse, hearing them start to speak in a tongue she did not recognise.

She tightened on grip on the machete as she watched her dead friend's head turn towards her and Susie.

Getting to her feet, Jenny's lips curved into a demonic smile.

Rachel looked in every direction, watching the circle of Vetala begin to constrict around her and Susie.

Chapter Ten

Releasing Susie's arm, Rachel raised the silver machete.

A hole appeared in Jenny's forehead when a gunshot sounded and her body collapsed for the second time. Another pair of shots and two more Vetala fell.

Seeing an opening in the circle, Rachel grabbed Susie's wrist and pulled her through the gap.

Catherine moved forward from her vantage point, stopping between the two girls and the circle of Vetala. "How fast can you run?"

Glancing as the Vetala began to advance towards them, Rachel raised the machete. "We're on the school track team."

Swinging the gun round, Catherine made the two teenagers duck as she fired at the Vetala by the gate. "Then go for the gold."

Rachel and Susie broke into a run as the Vetala by the gate went down.

Turning back, Catherine fired several more rounds before breaking into a sprint behind the two girls.

Passing them as the girls raced across to the other side of the road, she looked back as she veered to the right. "This way."

Intent on following her, Rachel and Susie continued running through the woods.

Stopping, Catherine took up a position behind a tree and raised her gun, aiming it at the few Vetala that were following.

A solitary Vetala lunged out of the darkness towards Catherine, the almost fleshless face appearing to grin as rotting fingers reached her throat.

The tip of Rachel's machete burst out through the Vetala's chest.

Pushing the demon inhabited corpse away, Catherine watched Rachel yank the blade from the decaying body after it collapsed. "Thanks, but get down."

Rachel dropped.

Raising her gun, Catherine fired at two more Vetala that were making for Susie, killing both of them with two rounds. "Get your friend."

Hearing another gunshot, Cutter pulled out the Smith & Wesson Sigma from his shoulder holster.

Walking to the other side of his van, he glanced back as Ian and Amanda jumped out from the other parked van. "Arm yourselves."

Raising the gun the instant he saw movement in the darkness, Cutter watched Catherine and the two girls come into view.

She looked the raised gun in his hand as she and the girls passed him, shaking her head. "We lost them a good ten minutes ago."

Cutter focused on the two girls, "And these are?"

"Rachel Shaw." She looked back at her friend, "That's Susie Brody." Rachel turned her attention towards Catherine, "And I know you're Catherine Jordan."

The mention of her name made her turn back towards the two girls, "How the hell do you know who I am?"

Rachel looked at Susie before answering, "One of my friends recognised you when you came to the school earlier." She looked at the still confused expression Catherine and Cutter were giving, "Our parents, all our parents work for the Trust one way or another. They sent us here to keep us out of the family business."

"You became hunters regardless." Amanda stepped forward.

Rachel nodded, "We're good at it." She held up the silver machete she had in her hand, "And we have the tools."

Snatching the machete from her, Catherine glared at Rachel. "You're just amateurs and you got your friend killed back there. Do you want to be the one to tell her parents how she died or how her body was possessed by a demon?" She glanced at Cutter, "I'm going to take these girls back to the school. While I'm gone, I want you to get an assault team down to the salt mines. Tell them we'll meet them there as soon as I've taken care of the girls."

"We want to help, we owe those Vetala some payback." Rachel tried to stare Catherine down.

Throwing the machete blade first at the girl's feet, Catherine stepped towards Rachel. "Do you want me to call your parents?" Watching the girl back down at the threat, she glanced away from Rachel and towards Susie. "Both of you, get moving. Back to school."

Ushering the two girls down the rough path from the top of the hill, Catherine remained close behind them.

Rachel turned her head and started to speak, but the glare from Catherine made her fall silent.

Reaching the bottom of the hill, Catherine watched the girls start towards the school building. "You're going to have to tell your teachers that your friend is just missing. They'll contact the police and it'll be arranged for her body to be found. You are not to tell anyone the truth."

Susie looked back, "What about our parents?"

"They'll get to know the truth and all of you are going to have to face the consequences of what you've been doing."

Emerging from the woods onto the edge of the school grounds, Rachel stopped at the sight of Myriam wandering aimlessly halfway across the perfectly cut lawn.

Recognising the uniform that the girl was wearing, Catherine halted next to Rachel and Susie. "She one of your little gang?"

Shaking her head in unison with her friend, Rachel answered first. "No."

Watching Myriam remove a bottle from the pocket of her school blazer, Catherine started to approach as the girl took a swig of the contents.

Myriam ignored her presence, letting her get close enough to identify the whiskey label on the bottle.

"She's drunk." Catherine looked back at Rachel and Susie, "Get her back inside."

Offering no resistance when the two girls took her arms, Myriam allowed them to begin pulling her towards the school.

Removing the mobile from her blazer pocket, Rachel dialled a number and lifted it to her ear. "We're on our way back, be ready to open the door."

"This is as far as I go."

Catherine's voice made Rachel turn, her fingers slipping from Myriam's arm. "You're not coming up to meet my team?"

"Your team?" Grabbing the girl's wrist, Catherine pulled Rachel out of the earshot of Myriam. "Proper field agents don't go blabbing about Trust business in front of civilians."

Rachel turned and looked at the nonchalant expression on Myriam's face, "She's seen you and she'll ask questions about us being out here, she might even tell the teachers."

"Lie to her, that's what a real operative would do. Now get her inside, put her to bed and hope she doesn't do anything to expose you."

Watching Catherine start walking away again, Rachel hurried back to help Susie take Myriam up the fire escape.

Seeing Rachel and Susie coming up the fire escape from the other side of the open fire door, Karen stepped out when she saw Myriam between them. "Where's Jenny?"

Rachel shook her head, glancing past Myriam at Susie. "Get her back to her room."

Half carrying Myriam to the door to her dorm room, Susie reached out and turned the handle. Entering the darkened room, she glanced at the sleeping form of Laura.

Almost dragging Myriam to the empty bed, Susie let her collapse on the mattress and turned back to the light from the passage.

Her head turning as Susie shut the door behind her, Myriam got up off her bed. Walking to the door, she pressed her palm against the wood.

Twisting her head to look across at Laura, she moved to the side of the bed. Reaching out, she clamped her hand down over the girl's mouth.

Laura's eyes opened and she began to instinctively struggle against the hand pressing against her lips.

Myriam slipped her other hand behind the back of the struggling girl's head and snapped Laura's neck.

Removing her hands, Myriam focused on Laura's blank expression and began to smile.

Chapter Eleven

Returning to the top of the hill, Catherine ejected the almost empty clip from her Ruger. She stopped when she reached Cutter's van, sliding open the side door.

Watching her select a full clip from a bag on the van floor, Cutter approached her. "What are you going to do about those girls?"

Slipping the fresh clip into her gun, Catherine looked at him. "Try to set up a meeting with their parents, I think the one in charge could be an exceptional operative with the right guidance. She kind of reminds me of myself at that age, minus my habit of getting expelled all the time."

"I can't imagine why you would get expelled." Cutter took a Benelli M3 shotgun from his van and checked it was loaded.

A grin appeared on her face, "Unladylike behaviour was the usual reason." Moving to the other van, Catherine placed her gun on the metal floor and picked up her holster, sliding it over her shoulder. She glanced towards Ian and Amanda as she slipped the Ruger into the holster, "I want you two to stay here. Keep an eye on the school and make sure none of those girls get any bright ideas about having a second shot at the Vetala."

"No problem." Ian stepped towards her and Cutter, "But you sure you don't want us coming with you?" He saw the expressions on their faces, "I know we've only been out of basic training a couple of weeks, but we're dying to see some action."

There was anger in Catherine's voice when she responded, "You think making sure those girls don't get themselves killed isn't important?"

Moving forward, Amanda slipped her hand under Ian's arm. "Don't listen to him, we're more than happy to stay here." She gave him a glaring look, "Aren't we, Ian?"

Watching him nod, Catherine opened the passenger door and climbed onto the seat. Pulling the door shut, she waited for Cutter to get behind the wheel.

Cutter started the engine and turned the van towards the muddy trail leading down to the road.

Pulling out her mobile from the back pocket of her jeans, Catherine turned it on and looked at the display. "No signal, looks like the assault team are already in position."

Turning at the bottom of the hill, Cutter took his eyes off the road for a brief moment to glance at Catherine. "Want to share the real reason you didn't want Ian and Amanda coming along?"

"I don't think he's ready yet." Catherine glanced out through the passenger window, "He's still too obsessed with what happened to his sister, payback is the only thing he's thinking about."

Cutter turned the van onto the road leading away from the lake, "I'm told you had a similar attitude when you and Forrest went after Stefano Balasi."

She snapped her head away from the window, spots of rain beginning to hit the glass. "I was going after bad guys long before what happened to Kate and I certainly hadn't just left high school." Catherine paused for a moment, "It occurs to me that you don't talk much about your past. You've never even mentioned if you have any family."

There was a delay before he answered, "I have a wife and a daughter, they're living in Boston." Cutter focused on the road ahead, turning on the windscreen wipers as the rain became more frequent. "I haven't seen them in a long time."

"This is the twenty first century, there's nothing to stop you popping over for a week or two."

Turning onto the road leading to the salt mine, he saw three parked vans coming into view after a few moments. "I can never go back."

Waiting for Cutter to bring the van to a stop, Catherine stepped out into the downpour, pulling the Ruger from her holster.

Reaching the nearest van, she peered through the glass at the two seats. Catherine glanced back at Cutter as he emerged from the van, watching him sling a heavy bag over his shoulder. "Empty."

Cutter pointed the barrel of his shotgun towards the open gate of the salt mine. "It's a little quiet." Taking the lead, he moved beyond the gate.

Staying close behind him, Catherine's eyes fell on Jenny's corpse, the rain soaking the dead girl's uniform. Moving ahead of Cutter, she stopped by the door to the nearest warehouse and peered inside.

The floor inside was littered with corpses in various stages of decomposition.

Entering with Cutter bringing up the rear, Catherine took a few steps towards the ramp leading down into the mine, slipping a pen thin torch from the pocket of her jeans.

The sound of gunfire coming from further inside the mine made her stop and glance back at Cutter, turning on the torch. "What are you waiting for? Aren't you going to do your chivalry thing and insist on going first?"

A slight smile appeared on his face, removing a much thicker torch from the bag over his shoulder. He attached the torch to a pair of hooks under the barrel of his shotgun, "I just got tired of seeing that look you're always giving me."

Descending the ramp ahead of him, Catherine stopped at the bottom and glanced along the passage. Hearing more gunfire and then silence, she looked at Cutter before starting along the tunnel.

A shape began to form ahead.

Catherine raised her Ruger and directed the torch into the darkness, watching the shape take form.

Emerging from the blackness in front of her, a man in body armour moved towards Catherine.

Standing behind her, Cutter raised the shotgun and aimed it at the back of her head. His finger tightening on the trigger, he watched the side of the man's head burst in a geyser of blood and brains.

Crouching down over the corpse, Catherine focused on the body armour that the man was wearing, spotting the empty space on the dead man's belt. "This looks bad."

"Do we press on?"

Catherine nodded, "These things need to be killed." Returning to her full height, she turned her attention to him. "We're also going to need one of the team's phones to get bypass the jamming signal."

Following her into the darkness, Cutter kept his shotgun fixed torch aimed beyond her, his finger remaining hovering over the trigger.

Catherine saw a dim light come into view as she continued round a bend in the tunnel, stopping after a few moments when another burst of gunfire erupted ahead.

Her pace increasing towards the light, she emerged onto a wooden platform just in time to see one of the assault team being thrust against a broken girder protruding from a pile of rusted scrap metal.

Firing off two rounds into the foreheads of the two Vetala responsible for the man's death, she watched them fall amidst the other corpses scattered across the chamber floor. Starting for the wooden steps leading down to the main floor of the chamber, she was grabbed from behind by a pair of hands devoid of flesh, the Ruger falling from her grasp.

Cutter grabbed for a lump of dirty blonde hair hanging from the head of Catherine's attacker, the skeletal face turning towards him.

The possessed corpse ripped the shotgun from his grasp, releasing the hold it had on Catherine.

Stopping the Vetala's fingers from reaching his throat, Cutter was slammed against the tunnel wall.

Grabbing the tattered clothing that the Vetala was wearing, Catherine shoved the corpse towards the wooden barricade at the edge of the platform.

The Vetala ripped the top plank of wood from the barricade and swung it round.

A protruding nail from the edge of the plank slashing her forehead, Catherine used the impact to give herself the momentum to swing round with her foot, catapulting the Vetala off the platform.

Recovering her gun, she stopped at the edge and aimed it at the fallen corpse. Pulling the trigger, she watched the Vetala jerk as the bullet broke through the skull.

She rushed down the wooden steps to the main floor, moving to where the soldier was impaled.

Unable to find a pulse at the side of his neck, she glanced back as Cutter descended from the platform. "He's gone."

Cutter looked at the bodies of the other soldiers among the Vetala possessed corpses, "So are the others." He gave the bodies a quick examination, noticing the broken electronics close to each of the corpses. "We're not going to be able to get the jamming signal turned off, these phones are nothing but junk." He glanced at the space beneath the platform, "Cat, you better look at this."

Turning her attention in the direction that he was looking, Catherine walked towards the table and focused on the mass of the photographs littering the surface. "It's the school." She picked up one of the pictures, looking back at Cutter. "Daph said these Vetala are attracted to people in power, the girls at the school are from influential and rich families. What if getting to the girls was their plan all along?"

Slipping her Ruger into her shoulder holster, Catherine glanced at the corpses. "The team has been slaughtered, right?" She watched Cutter nod, "Then where are the Vetala that did this?"

"The assault could have made them advance their timetable and if there's another way out, they could already be on the way to the school." He glanced at the dead Vetala, "These were probably left to summon more Vetala to possess the team."

Catherine collected two of the discarded P90s from the floor, "If you're right, someone's going to have to try to slow them down and someone has to prepare everyone at the school in case I don't make it."

"You've decided you'll be the one trying to delay them." Cutter followed her back up to the platform, "You've got someone in your life, I haven't. Makes more sense for me to go."

She gave him a stern look, glancing back as she started into the tunnel. "That's why you shouldn't, you've got nothing to lose."

Chapter Twelve

Angela closed the door to her private room and started towards the stairs leading down.

Descending to the ground floor, she pushed her way through the nearest door into the school kitchen.

Passing the staff preparing the multitude of breakfasts, she walked through the other into the dining hall.

She stopped halfway towards the staff table, her gaze turning towards the other entrance. Seeing Laura entering with Myriam behind her, she made her way past the rows of tables to reach her daughter.

Walking straight past her, Laura ignored her and continued to the same table that Myriam was heading for.

"Don't I even merit a good morning?"

Laura continued walking.

Reaching out, Angela caught hold of her daughter's arm. "Look at me when I'm talking to you."

Turning, Laura glared at her mother. "Leave me alone."

Angela glanced at the staring faces of the students and staff, her expression turning to anger as she returned her gaze towards her daughter. "Don't you dare talk to me like that."

"Let me go." Laura pulled herself from her mother's grasp, "The others are waiting."

There was complete silence in the dining hall, everyone waiting for Angela's response.

"I want you in my office as soon as you've finished your breakfast." Angela gave Laura one last threatening look, "Don't even think about disobeying me."

Laura made no attempt to respond as she turned back and continued to the table where Myriam was sitting with three other girls.

Watching her daughter take her place at the empty table, Angela glanced at all the faces staring at her. Trying to remain composed as she turned away, she took deliberately slow steps in her exit from the dining hall.

Cradling the two P90s on her lap as Cutter parked the van, Catherine looked at Ian and Amanda framed in the headlights.

Getting out, she stepped into the glare. "You're going with Cutter down to the school."

Amanda saw the blood under the gash on Catherine's forehead, "What happened?"

Glancing back as Cutter began filling several large holdalls with weapons from the van, she urgently redirected her focus to Ian and Amanda. "The Vetala are coming, you have to make sure the school is protected. I'll be buying you as much time as I can."

She remained watching as the three of them began scrambling down the hill with the weapon filled holdalls.

Turning, Catherine raised the two P90s and started in the opposite direction. Managing to keep her balance going down the other side of the hill, she glimpsed the walking corpses lurching towards her.

Raising the two weapons, she glanced all around as the Vetala began appearing from every direction.

Rushing down the stairs towards the main door when she heard the hammering from outside, Angela unbolted it and started to pull it open.

Cutter pushed the door open the rest of the way and hurried inside, pointing the barrel of the shotgun towards the teacher. "We're not going to hurt anyone."

Entering behind him, Ian and Amanda removed automatic pistols from the holdalls.

"Find the girl that was hunting the Vetala." Waiting until Amanda started up the stairs, Cutter turned his attention back to Ian. "Secure the door, do your best to ensure it holds."

Angela watched Ian push the door shut, her gaze drifting back to the gun still being aimed at her. "What do you people want?"

"Trying to keep everyone in this school alive." Cutter looked at the two girls coming from the dining hall, watching the fear appear on their faces when they saw his shotgun. "You don't need to be afraid of us, we're here to protect you."

Positioning herself between Cutter and the girls, Angela started to slowly urge them back towards the passage leading to the dining hall.

"It's okay, Ms Graham."

She looked towards the stairs at Rachel, Karen and several other girls coming down with Amanda at the rear.

Reaching the bottom of the stairs, Rachel looked at Amanda and back towards Cutter. "You going to let us fight with you?"

Karen pushed her way to the front of the group, "I thought Catherine Jordan would be with you, I wanted to ask..."

"We don't have time for pointless questions." Cutter glanced at the door, "You girls need to make sure all the ways in are secure." He turned back towards the group, "If the Vetala get inside, it's going to be a massacre."

Letting her friends depart without her, Rachel unzipped one of the holdalls and pulled out a P90. "This is so cool." She looked up at the horrified expression appearing on Angela's face, "It's all right, Ms Graham. I know what I'm doing."

Angela watched Rachel continue handling the weapon, "Will someone tell me what is going on?"

"She's your teacher." Cutter gave Rachel an impatient glare, "Explain it to her."

Standing up with the P90 in her grip, she looked at Angela. "The corporation my Dad runs, it's just a cover to raise funds to help these people." Rachel pointed towards the three hunters, "He and my Mum used to be just like them." She turned back to focus on Angela's face, hesitant to reveal the rest. "My parents, they used to hunt demons."

"I don't what sort of nonsense you're involved in." Angela removed the phone from the inside of her jacket, "I'm calling the police, I'll let them sort out these fantasies."

Rachel looked at the teacher's expression when she was unable to get a signal, "Figured that would happen." She looked back at Cutter, "It is still the way things are done, phone lines blocked?"

He nodded, turning his attention back to Angela. "I know all this is difficult to believe, but I'm going to ask that you trust us. We are the good guys."

Angela slipped the phone back into her jacket pocket, a defiant expression filling her face. "I'll use the one in my office."

Starting for the archway by the stairs, she stopped when more hammering on the door began.

"It could be Cat." Ian moved towards the door, his hand reaching out for the thick bolt.

Watching Cutter raise his shotgun, Rachel did the same with the P90. "This is loaded with silver rounds, isn't it?"

The door starting to open before she got an answer, she caught a glimpse of rotting flesh as it was pushed from the outside.

Flung the rest of the way open, the door smashed Ian back.

Rachel's finger squeezed the trigger of the P90, seeing the Vetala enter the hall.

No rounds came out of the weapon.

Firing the shotgun, Cutter watched the first Vetala fall, several cockroaches crawling out from the remains of the rotted flesh.

He made for the door.

Amidst the screaming of the two girls standing behind Angela as another pair of flesh peeling corpses came through the open doorway, Rachel saw one of them grab Cutter's shotgun and slam him against the wall. She gave up trying to shoot the P90 and swung it like a club, smashing it against the head of the other Vetala.

Pushed away, Rachel slammed down onto the tiled floor, the weapon falling from her grasp.

The Vetala that pushed her made for Angela and shoved her aside, the near flesh covered hands reaching for one of the screaming girls.

By the time Rachel's fingers retrieved the P90, she had heard the snapping of the girl's neck. Trying to rise in time to save the other, she raised the P90 to swing it at the back of the Vetala's head.

The back of the Vetala's body erupted with little geysers of decayed flesh.

Watching the corpse fall, Rachel swung her head towards the open door.

Catherine let loose with the second P90 in her possession, firing the rounds at the Vetala that was still struggling with Cutter.

Pushing the now lifeless corpse away, Cutter hurried to the door and slammed it shut. Locking it, he turned towards Catherine. "We have to be sure you're not one of them."

"I'd be worried if you didn't." Catherine let him check her pulse.

Cutter turned his attention to Rachel, watching her fiddling with the P90. "Next time, remember to take the safety off."

Becoming aware of Angela's glare, Catherine looked at her. "I apologise for my team's presence." She glanced at the corpses, "But there's more of these things on the way, they're only a few minutes behind me." She redirected her gaze towards the teacher, "They will slaughter all of your students if they get inside."

"My daughter." Angela focused on the body of the girl that had been killed during the attack, her gaze eventually rising to lock with Catherine's eyes.

Abandoning the surviving girl that was still cowering behind her, she rushed up the stairs and headed for the dorm rooms.

She reached the room that Myriam and Laura were assigned to. Her hand gripping the handle, she turned it and started to push the door open.

The drawn curtains kept the room dark.

Stepping into the room, Angela approached the curtains and opened them. She froze when she looked through the window.

Dozens of corpses were stood on the gravel covering the front of the school building.

Backing away from the window, she heard footsteps behind her.

Forcing herself to take her eyes off the view from the window, she began to turn.

"Don't get too worried, we've made sure all the doors are locked and bolted." Amanda entered the room, "They're not getting in."

Angela looked back through the window, "What are they?"

Moving forward, Amanda stopped next to her. "They call themselves Vetala. Basically they're demons that can be summoned to inhabit anyone who's dead."

"And you fight them?"

Amanda nodded, "Them and other things. I spent years at a special school learning all about them and how to kill them."

Footsteps in the passage outside made Angela turn towards several girls passing the open door, the reason for her coming to the room returning to the forefront of her mind. "I have to find my daughter."

"Cat and the others probably could use your help, so I'll tell you what I'll do. I'll find your daughter and bring her to you." Amanda glanced around the room, "It would be helpful if I had a picture."

Angela moved to the chest of drawers at the foot of Laura's bed and opened the one at the bottom. Reaching under the pile of underwear, she pulled out a framed picture. "Will this do, it's a few years old I'm afraid?"

Taking it from her, Amanda looked at Angela and Laura hugging each other with smiles on their faces. "You look very happy together."

There was a delay in Angela's response, "It was taken before I divorced her father." She saw Amanda's inquisitive expression, "He still lives in Sydney. Laura's never forgiven me for moving here when I was offered this position."

"I'm sure you'll get the chance to work things out." Amanda placed the picture on the top of the chest of drawers, "I'll find your daughter, don't worry."

Chapter Thirteen

Turning off the tap, Catherine finished washing the blood from the side of her face. Glancing back as the door opened, she watched Rachel enter and stop by one of the toilet stalls.

The teenager gave Catherine a wide grin, "I know she's not supposed to, but my Mum let me read copies of all your case files. I guess what I want to say is I think you kick ass."

"I hope you're not looking for an autograph."

Rachel shook her head, "I just really admire you and everything you've done. All the demons you've killed, taking on Countess Bathory." She paused for a brief moment, "Oh, the Lamia on Fog Island, don't forget that."

"I've also lost friends. Poppy, Jenna. They were all lost doing this job." Catherine dropped the blood stained paper towel into a bin, "I even almost lost my girlfriend not so long ago." She walked towards Rachel, "One golden rule you need to remember, this job can cost us the lives of the people we care about."

Approaching the closed door, Daphne removed the key from her pocket and pushed it into the lock.

She opened the door and stepped inside Catherine's apartment. Pausing by the couch for a moment, she continued towards the door to the main bedroom.

Heading inside, she stared at the neatly made bed. Venturing further into the bedroom, she picked up the phone on the cabinet at the side of the bed.

Daphne typed in a number and raised it to her ear, "It's Daphne, I'm worried about Catherine. She didn't come back to my place last night and she isn't at her apartment." She moved to the bed and sat down,

"Forrest, she hasn't even called to let me know she's okay and that's no like her." Her head turned towards the window, "Okay, I'll meet you there."

Pushing open the rusted door, Cutter stepped out onto the roof with Catherine and Rachel close behind.

Reaching the edge, he glanced down at the yard. "They don't seem to be doing much, do they?"

Rachel stopped at his side and leaned forward, peering down at the motionless Vetala scattered around the front of the school, "That's a good thing." She looked back at Catherine, "Right?"

"Why don't you go check the other sides, see if any are trying to get in through any of the other doors." Catherine waited for Rachel to nod and begin heading for the far side of the roof, turning her attention back to Cutter. "Daph told me these things were smart, so why aren't they attacking? They can't know that we don't have any backup on the way."

"Perhaps some of them are already inside." Cutter was the first to turn towards the other side of the roof at the sound of a brief burst of gunfire.

Following him to where Rachel was standing, Catherine saw the ecstatic expression on the girl's face. "What do you think you're doing?"

Rachel looked down at the sprawled out corpse lying on the grass at the rear of the building, tightening her grip on the P90. "This gun is so cool."

"Stay here and keep an eye on our friends below." Catherine focused on Rachel, "You're coming with me, we've got to get your friends ready for what's coming.

Watching the plump girl point towards the single door in the passage ahead, Amanda thanked her and started along the passage.

Pushing the door open, she stepped onto the hard tiled floor of the school gym. Hearing voices coming from beyond a door on the far wall as she got closer, she raised the Sig in her hand and aimed the barrel towards the door.

She kept the gun level as she turned the handle on the door and pushed it open.

Laura and three other girls twisted their heads to look at her as she entered the large store room full of sports equipment.

Amanda was about to speak when she saw the stretched out body of another girl with her lifeless eyes staring up towards the ceiling.

Her finger beginning to squeeze the trigger, she felt something hard smash down against the back of her head.

Watching Amanda fall, Myriam released the hockey stick she was holding and reached down. Both her hands gripping either side of Amanda's head, she pulled until she heard the snapping of bone. "Prepare her, she will be next."

Chapter Fourteen

Reaching the stairs leading to the entrance hall, Catherine started down, watching Karen begin looking at her.

Stepping away from the group that Ian was showing how to use a P90, Karen approached Catherine. "My Mum was murdered by Stefano Balasi. I was told she was in one of your homeless shelters when she was killed, the one in London."

"You're talking about Frieda Jolanka." She watched the girl nod, "I didn't know she was undercover until after she was gone."

Karen wiped a tear from her cheek, "Thanks for being honest."

"I imagine she would want you to survive what's to come." Catherine handed her spare P90 to the girl, "Can you handle one of these?"

Nodding, Karen flicked off the safety. "Sure thing."

"I want you to take over showing the other girls how to use them until we get back." She glanced at Ian and Rachel, "We're going to make another sweep of the school, make sure all the exterior doors are locked and bolted."

Pausing only to reload her P90 with a full clip, Catherine started along the passage leading to the dining hall with Ian and Rachel moving to follow her.

Catherine reached the dining hall door and pushed it open. Entering first, she began walking between the rows of tables, her eyes focused on the door to the kitchen on the far wall.

Stopping in the middle of the room, Rachel watched Catherine raise her weapon. "They're still outside, right?"

"Quiet." Getting closer to the kitchen door, Catherine prodded it with the barrel of her P90.

Letting Ian see the concern on her face, Rachel watched Catherine start to enter.

Sweeping the kitchen with weapon as she entered, Catherine ventured along the tiled floor. She stopped between a long metal table and a row of three extra large refrigerators, glancing at the door leading outside to check it was still bolted.

Moving round the table, she glanced back for a moment to check Ian and Rachel had entered the kitchen and pointed her gun towards a door on the other wall. "Where's that lead?"

"Just the basement." Rachel started towards the door.

Raising her free hand to stop the girl from getting any closer, Catherine pointed to the drops of blood on the tile nearest to the door.

Rachel came to a sudden stop, the gun in her hand beginning to rise.

Her fingers gripping the handle, Catherine began to turn it. Waiting until she made sure both Ian and Rachel had their weapons ready, she pulled the door open and aimed the barrel of her P90 into the darkness.

Reaching for the light switch with her free hand, she focused on the splatters of blood leading down the concrete steps when the bulb flickered on.

"Better stay up here." Catherine started down the steps, aiming her gun towards the bottom.

Reaching the basement floor, she turned towards the stack of washing machines on the far wall. Hearing a low voice from the other side of a door sized opening in the wall, she began moving towards it.

Catherine's gaze focused on the bodies of the kitchen staff dumped on the concrete floor as she stepped through into the adjacent room.

Catching a glimpse of movement, she began to turn.

Her gaze fixated on the open door, Rachel jerked a little when she heard the brief gunfire coming from the basement.

The moment the gunfire stopped, she turned her eyes towards Ian. "Shouldn't we..."

Ian cut her off, "Cat wanted us to stay here." He looked at the fear appearing on her face, "She knows what she is doing."

"But..." She fell silent again, hearing the sound of the door to the dining hall beginning to open.

Turning her head towards the door, Rachel saw one of the younger pupils coming inside, lowering her weapon. "It's okay, it's Geri. She's a friend."

Rachel hurried to the other side of the table, leaving Ian to stare suspiciously at the young girl.

Lashing out with a pair of scissors concealed behind her back, the girl almost connected the bladed tip with Rachel's chest.

Catherine pushed Ian to one side when she reached the top of the basement steps, firing a single shot into the girl's forehead.

The door moved again, pushing against the corpse.

"Get clear." Catherine waited for Rachel to step back and fired at the door, the wood erupting as the rounds ripped through to the other side.

Hurrying round the table, she pushed the door open and aimed the P90 into the dining hall.

The number of walking corpses on the other side of the door made her let it swing shut. "Back, down to the cellar."

Pushing Rachel ahead of her, Catherine turned as she followed Ian down the steps. Firing the P90 at the first few Vetala entering the kitchen, she backed through the basement door.

Grabbing the door handle, she slammed it shut and hurried to the bottom of the steps.

Turning when she reached the floor, she crouched and aimed her weapon towards the top of the steps.

Chapter Fifteen

"Perhaps we should go back and check the dorm rooms again? She might have run into one of the girls we've been sending back there."

Angela closed the door to the classroom when she heard Jessica's comment, her head beginning to tilt into a nod.

The sound of distant gunfire stopped from her answering.

Hurrying to the door on the opposite wall, she pushed it open and rushed to the row of windows to see what was happening. She stopped and looked down at the schoolyard, "There's dozens of them now."

Jessica followed her and focused on all the motionless Vetala massed below for several moments. She was about to respond when she saw one of the doors open, fear appearing in her voice. "Someone's letting them in."

Laura stepped out into the yard, moving aside to allow the possessed corpses to enter.

"Oh God." Angela backed away from the window, her hands cupping her mouth. "She's helping them?"

Turning away from the window, Jessica started to make an urgent dash for the door. "We've got to tell those people."

Angela did not move, tears beginning to form. "They must have tricked her into letting them in."

"I know you don't want to hear this, Angie." Jessica halted by the door, "They must have made her one of them."

Shaking her head wildly, Angela expression turned to anger, the tears streaming down her cheeks. "My daughter is not one of those things, she is not dead. They're just forcing her to help them, that's all."

Another burst of gunfire made Jessica peer back out into the passage.

Two girls stepped into view at the far end of the corridor, their heads turning to look straight at Jessica.

Watching them start advancing towards her, Jessica got an unpleasant feeling from the way the girls were looking at her. "They're coming."

Angela made no attempt to move, "I don't care."

Rushing back into the classroom, Jessica grabbed Angela's arm and started to lead her towards the door.

Offering no resistance, Angela pulled her arm free when she reached the corridor. She started to walk towards the approaching girls, letting loose with her rage. "Why is my daughter helping you?"

The girls continued to walk towards them.

"Get down."

The sound of Cutter's voice made Jessica push Angela against the corridor wall.

The two girls collapsing as rounds from Cutter's shotgun ripped into their bodies, Jessica shoved Angela towards him.

Moving past them when another Vetala appeared at the other end of the passage, Cutter fired at the possessed girl and watched her fall. "Back the other way."

Jessica urged Angela to start moving, hearing him firing more rounds.

Turning her head to look back, she saw more girls moving towards Cutter, her fingers losing their grip on Angela's arm.

Making a dash for the other end of the passage, Angela passed the small alcove with the ladders leading up to a narrow ledge in front of a closed door.

She came to a stop when she saw the decaying corpses advancing from the adjacent corridor.

Rushing to go after her, Jessica watched her remain still as one of the Vetala reached the window she was standing next to.

The Vetala gripping Angela by the sides of her head, the possessed corpse smashed her face through the glass.

Screaming, Jessica watched the girl press Angela's throat down onto a shard of still standing glass.

"You can't help her." Cutter grabbed Jessica's arm and began pulling her away as Angela's body remained propped up by the window.

Pushed towards the alcove, Jessica looked back as he fired another round at one of the approaching Vetala.

"Up."

Jessica did as she was told and began scrambling to the narrow platform at the top of the ladder.

Stepping from the rung and onto the ledge, she pulled back the bolt and pushed against the door.

Falling onto the roof, she scraped her bare knees on the surface, scrambling away from the open door.

Cutter fired another round at one of the advancing Vetala and made for the ladder. Hurrying to the top, he felt fingers wrap around his ankle.

Looking down at the face of the teenager trying to drag him back, he aimed the barrel of the shotgun straight at her face and pulled the trigger.

He started towards the top of the ladder before the corpse fell.

Leaping forward onto the roof, he rolled onto his back on impact and aimed his shotgun towards the top of the ladder.

Cutter fired at the first head that came into view.

Watching from behind him, Jessica saw the girl's face vanished in a flash of blood.

Getting to his feet, Cutter continued to keep the shotgun aimed at the open doorway.

Her gaze remaining focused on the ladder, Jessica waited for another head to pop up, staring at the top rung for what seemed like an endless minute.

"What are they waiting for?"

Listening to the nervousness in her voice, Cutter took a step forward, leaning over the edge to peer down to the floor below.

All he saw was the body of the girl lying at the bottom of the ladder.

Taking a step back, he began removing several extra rounds from the pocket of his jacket. "We have to be ready for what they'll try next, they won't give up that easily."

Chapter Sixteen

Driving her Beetle into the car park beneath the amusement park, Daphne stopped near the four parked vans, glancing through the windscreen at the squad of armed soldiers in front of them.

Emerging from behind one of the vans as she got out of her car, Forrest slipped his Glock into the shoulder holster under his jacket. "We were almost ready to leave without you." He looked towards one of the soldiers, "Ricky is practically chomping at the bit to get some action."

Walking to the other side of her car, Daphne reached into glove box and removed a Makarov. Slipping it into jacket pocket, she started for the van nearest to Forrest. "Can we get going?"

The armed soldiers began getting into the vans.

Climbing behind the wheel of one of the vans, Forrest turned the key in the ignition, waiting until Daphne slipped into the seat next to him.

Starting to drive towards the exit from the underground car park, he slammed on the brakes when Vladek stopped in front of the van, the security barrier coming down behind him.

Forrest lowered the window and leaned out, "Could you step over to the side? We're in a hurry."

"I'm afraid I cannot allow this little excursion, Agent King. Please exit your vehicles."

Climbing out, Forrest looked back as the squad members exited the vans behind him. "Cat could be in trouble." He watched Daphne getting out, "Get that barrier up."

Vladek glanced at the members of the assault squad, "Colonel McCall, there is another situation that requires you and your team." He turned back towards Forrest, "As for you, Agent King. It has been brought to my attention that a pair of American students camping out on the Yorkshire Moors have been attacked. I would like you to go out there and find what is responsible. There's a contact at the Slaughtered Lamb inn you might want to talk to."

"You're going to have find someone else to do it." Forrest glanced long enough at Daphne to see her nod, "We're going to find Cat and Cutter." His expression became threatening, "Now raise that barrier or do we drive straight through it?"

Vladek started to step to one side, "It amazes me that you have so little regard for the talents of Agents Jordan and Smith." He stopped once he was away from the front of the van, signalling for the barrier to be raised. "Can it be that you don't trust them to handle whatever situation they are in by themselves? Agent Smith is a former Seal and Agent Jordan." A slight smile appeared on his face, "Well, let us just agree that she knows what it is like to kill and is proficient at the taking of human lives."

"Daph, get back in the van." Giving her a quick glance, Forrest returned his focus to Vladek. "I have no idea who you are." He climbed back behind the wheel, looking at Vladek as he pulled the door shut. "But I will find out."

Remaining motionless, Vladek watched the single van drive out onto the street.

Looking at Ian covering the steps to the school basement with his P90, Catherine leaned on one of the washing machines.

"It is going to be all right, isn't it?" Rachel watched her turn, "We will get out of this alive?"

Catherine glanced at her watch, "My friends are probably on the way here by now." She moved closer to the teenager, "And I imagine Daph and Forrest will be bringing reinforcements with them. I'd also like to believe that Cutter and Amanda are still alive."

Bowing her head, Rachel focused on the floor. "This isn't fun anymore." She raised her head and looked at Catherine, "This is all my fault, if I hadn't been such an asshole in wanting to take out the Vetala in the first place..."

Catherine interrupted her, "No, you're not to blame. The Vetala were always going to be coming here and if you and you're friends hadn't been hunting them, we would never have found out what they were planning."

"All my friends." The thought of them lingered in her mind, "They're probably dead and are walking around with those things inside them." Rachel looked back at Catherine, an expression of confusion on her face. "How do you deal with doing this every day?"

"You remember the victims. The ones we lose and more importantly the ones we save." She was about to continue when the sound of gunfire from the kitchen cut her off.

Rushing to the bottom of the steps, she gave Ian a quick glance. "Keep me covered."

Starting up towards the open door at the top, Catherine took each step slow.

She was halfway when she stopped, the P90 in her hands beginning to rise.

The girl in the school uniform at the top of the stairs froze, splashes of blood on her face visible in the light from the kitchen.

"I've found them."

Catherine saw the blood covered silver dagger in the girl's hand, "You've been busy." She glanced down the stairs as Rachel came into view, stopping her from rushing up towards her friend. She turned back towards the girl at the top of the stairs, "Tell me your name."

"Karen, Karen Jolanka."

Catherine lowered her P90, "I had to check you were still you." Moving past Karen, she stepped into the kitchen and looked at the bodies on the floor, then at the three girls armed with P90s. She turned back towards Karen, "You did all this?"

Walking to the kitchen sink, Karen turned on the tap and washed the blood from the knife she was carrying. "Yeah, we did."

Moving next to her, Catherine focused on the knife. "That silver?"

Karen nodded, "My mother gave it to me."

Hearing Ian and Rachel coming up from the basement, Catherine looked at the other girls. "None of you ever split up, even for a minute or two?"

One of the girls answered quickly, "No, Miss."

"That's not completely true." Karen glanced back at Catherine, "I did have to use the bathroom, I was alone until I was done." She looked at her friends, "They waited outside."

Catherine glanced at the three girls, "Do you mind?" Reaching out, she took each of her hands and felt for a pulse. "They're okay." She glanced over at Ian and Rachel, "Go make sure the hall is clear, we've got to try to reach the dorm rooms. There could be more students trapped there who are still alive." She looked back at Karen, "And there's no way I'm leaving anyone behind. You know the layout of the school, why don't you suggest the best route."

"I suppose we could try going through the library upstairs, there are two ways in but one is close to the dorm rooms." Karen looked at Rachel, "What do you think?"

Rachel gave a quick nod, "Beats taking the long way."

Moving to the dining hall door, Catherine pushed it open a little and peered through. "It's clear."

Heading to the other door, Karen turned her head to look back. "It's quicker through here."

"Sure, lead the way." Catherine moved away from the dining hall door, "Ian, you bring up the rear."

Letting Rachel and the other three girls follow Karen out of the kitchen, Ian saw the expression on Catherine's face as she approached. "What's wrong?"

She kept her voice low when she answered to avoid the girls overhearing her, "I'll tell you later." Stepping out into the passage, she walked past the row of girls, stopping when she reached Karen. "Are you waiting for something?"

"Sorry." Starting to move, Karen was almost at the corner when Catherine's fingers grabbed her arm.

Stopping the girl from continuing, Catherine passed her and raised the P90. Pausing just before turning the corner, she leaned forward to peer along the next corridor.

A dark haired teenager was next to a rotting corpse, both of them standing by a flight of stairs.

Catherine tightened her grip on the gun, "Get ready to move as soon as I take them out."

Stepping into their line of sight, she let loose with the P90, the multiple rounds ripping into their bodies.

Rushing out first, Karen tripped and started to fall close to one of the fallen corpses.

One of the girls following her reached down to help her to her feet.

Reacting at the sound of a door opening, Catherine redirected the barrel of the P90 towards the Vetala lunging out from one of the classrooms.

Jerking from the impact of the rounds from Catherine's weapon, the Vetala possessed woman slashed out with a kitchen knife, the long blade slicing into the girl's throat.

Watching the girl helping Karen collapse with blood squirting from where her throat had been cut open, Catherine stopped when Karen thrust her dagger into the chest of the walking corpse.

Catherine moved when the Vetala fell, coming to a stop by the fallen girl. Pressing her fingers against the blood, she was unable to find a pulse on the girl's neck. "Damn."

Her attention drifted almost instantly to the open door to the classroom. Hurrying to the doorway, she let loose with more rounds from her P90, slaughtering the occupants.

Catherine turned back to the rest of the group, "Go."

Remaining at the back of the group, Ian saw more Vetala possessed corpses appear at the far end of the passage. "Cat, we've got dead girls walking."

Dropping to his knee, he began firing his P90.

The first row of Vetala falling, Catherine clamped her hand down on his shoulder. "Save your bullets and get the girls up to the library, I'll hold them off."

"We're not going without you." Rachel pushed past Karen and the other two girls, "No one gets left behind, that's what you said."

Catherine fired a single round and watched the closest Vetala fall, her focus remaining on the others that were still advancing. "I'm going to be right behind you."

Retreating to the stairs, Ian started urging the girls up to the next floor. He gave Catherine a last look, "Good luck."

He raced up the stairs, hearing another burst of gunfire from Catherine's P90.

Stopping at the corner to another passage, Ian

saw Rachel and the other girls standing by the doors to the school library. "Let me check it's clear first."

Raising her P90 as he passed her, Rachel aimed the barrel towards the stairs.

The bursts of gunfire from the floor below stopped, followed by the sound of a brief scuffle.

Hearing footsteps on the steps, Rachel's finger began to tighten on the trigger.

A shadow appeared on the floor in front of the stairs.

Rachel saw the figure come into view and fired.

Chapter Seventeen

Rachel released her finger as the body fell, blood beginning to spread across the white school shirt the dead girl was wearing.

Rushing up from the ground floor, Catherine spun round as her back slammed against the wall opposite the stairs, firing at the Vetala coming up behind her. "Move it, into the library now."

The order made Rachel dash for the double doors being held open by the other girls.

Releasing several more rounds, Catherine rushed to the doors, pushing the girls holding them open inside.

The doors closing behind her, she turned. "Hold them shut."

Rachel and the other girls rushed forward, bracing themselves against the doors.

Glancing around the library, she hurried to one of the school computers, placing her P90 on the table next to it. Removing the plug from the wall socket, she lifted it off the table and carried to the door.

Placing the computer on the floor, Catherine started wrapping the plug cord around the door handles.

"Back away." She kept the P90 levelled at the doors, watching them move until the tied cord stopped them from opening any further. "That'll hold them for a while."

The Vetala began hammering on the doors.

Karen stopped by the table where Catherine had left her gun.

Returning from the other side of the library, "Cat, the other door. It's locked."

Glimpsing Karen standing by the table, Catherine retrieved her gun and started towards the other double doors.

She gave the lock a quick once over and glanced back at the girls, "Get one of the tables and bring it over here."

Moving to the table closest to her, Rachel waited until her friends joined her. Lifting it together, the girls carried it towards the doors.

"Should make a decent battering ram." Catherine moved until the table was between her and the doors. "Be careful, we don't know what's on the other side." She nodded, "Do it."

Raising the P90, Catherine stood motionless as the girls began slamming the table against the doors.

The banging on the other doors ceased.

Looking back, Catherine watched Ian start towards the double doors tied with the plug lead.

A brief burst of gunfire sounded from the other side.

There was a moment of complete silence.

"Let me in."

Ian glanced back at Catherine, "It's..." He fell silent when he watched her shake her head.

Walking back to the other side of the library, Catherine passed Ian and stopped by the doors. "What's your name?" She glanced back at Ian when there was no response, the banging starting again after a few moments of silence. "If the thing in Amanda's body tries to get through those doors, put a bullet in her head."

He watched her walk past him, "Just like that?"

Looking back, Catherine nodded. "Amanda is dead and you can mourn her later. For now you remember that is not her." She returned to where the girls were still holding the table, "Keep at it."

The wood on the doors beginning to splinter from the repeated impact of the table, she saw the lock buckle and raised her P90.

Thrusting the table against the doors one last time, the girls moved away as the doors swung open.

Catherine aimed her P90 at the passage beyond, beginning to move. Reaching the open doors, she stepped through to the other side.

Turning to make sure the corridor was clear, she glanced back towards the door to the dorm wing.

Rachel rushed out of the library and made straight for the door, hammering on the wood as she stopped in front of it. "It's me, Rachel. Let us in."

Leaving the library, Karen heard the bolts on the other side of the door being pulled back.

The door to the school dorm rooms opening from the other side, Rachel began to turn towards Catherine.

Karen started to move, the blade of her knife pointed towards Catherine.

Rushing forward, Rachel grabbed the shoulder of Karen's school blazer, spinning the girl round to face her.

The blade ripped into the front of Rachel's uniform, blood immediately spreading over the fabric.

Chapter Eighteen

Rachel falling as the knife was ripped out of her chest with a gush of blood, Catherine gripped Karen's wrist and pushed her towards Ian. "Get that thing into the dorms." Focusing her attention back towards Rachel, she knelt over the girl and looked at the red stain soaking the shirt.

Sliding her hands beneath Rachel's body, she lifted her and started towards the open door. Passing through the frame, she made for the nearest dorm room.

Entering, Catherine lowered Rachel onto the bed.

Rachel winced as she was laid out, breathing heavily. "It hurts."

Catherine let the girl see her smile, "You're going to be fine, trust me. Just hold on a little longer and when you're patched up, I'll recommend you for field training myself. You'll be out there kicking ass before you know it."

The girl coughed, managing to focus once more on Catherine's face as she struggled to smile. "I'll make a great agent, wait and see."

"I know you will. But for now, you just stay still. I'll be back as soon as I can." Returning to the passage, she glanced at Karen. "I was never fooled by your act."

Her arms restrained by Ian and one of the other girls, Karen appeared defiant as she looked at Catherine. "It doesn't matter. None of you will survive, we will have your bodies."

Catherine backed away, "Get away from that thing."

The venomous tone in her voice made Ian and the girl release Karen's arms, moving away rapidly.

She raised the P90 and kept her finger pressed down on the trigger.

There were several screams as the front of Karen's body erupted with a multitude of red geysers until she fell.

Lowering the weapon when she was done, Catherine glanced back at the dorm room where she had placed Rachel. "I suppose it's too much to hope anyone here has any first aid training."

There was nothing but silence.

Walking towards the fire exit, she glanced back along the passage. "That leads outside, right?"

"Yeah." Susie stepped away from a group of armed girls, "That's how we got out the nights we went hunting, no one ever saw us."

Ian moved towards Catherine, "What are you going to do?"

"I'm going to get one of the vans, bring it back and get Rachel to where she can get medical help." She removed the clip from her P90 and checked the number of remaining rounds, glancing towards Susie. "Where do you keep the weapons you were using?"

"Rachel's room." Susie looked at one of open doors, "She keeps them in her locker."

Hurrying towards the room that the girl was looking at, Catherine saw the locker next to the bed. Entering, she knelt down and glanced back as Susie stopped in the doorway. "The key, where is it?"

"Rachel always kept it on her." Susie saw the expression on Catherine's face, "I'll go get it."

Running to the room where Rachel had been taken, Susie approached the bed and saw the blood soaking her friend's shirt. She reached inside the blazer and removed the key. Pulling her hand back, she looked at Rachel's blood on her skin.

Susie took a final look at the face of her friend and rushed back to Catherine, "Here."

Snatching the key from the girl's fingers in her rush to open the locker, Catherine released the padlock and raised the lid.

"This is quite the arsenal."

Susie peered over Catherine's shoulder at the assortment of different sized blades and a pair of Glocks, "Rachel's brother works at the Trust armoury depot in Glasgow, he got her all this. He wanted her to be safe."

Selecting a large silver bladed knife, Catherine also grabbed one of the guns, checked the clip was full of silver tipped rounds and shoved it into the back of her jeans. Collecting the knife, she closed the lid and stood up, turning to face Susie. "You should be with Rachel."

Exiting the room, Catherine walked towards the fire exit.

Ian followed her to the thick door, "Sure you want to do this?"

"She won't make it if I don't." She pushed down the level to open the door and stepped onto the metal platform, looking back inside. "Do whatever it takes to protect these girls."

Catherine pushed the door shut, turning as footsteps sounded on the metal steps.

Pulling out the gun from the back of her jeans with one hand, she tightened the grip on the dagger with her other and focused on the Vetala coming up the fire escape.

As soon as the first possessed corpse came within reach, she lashed out with the blade, slicing through the rotting flesh.

Catherine kicked the body down the steps, watching the others move to avoid the corpse rolling towards them.

Shooting two more in the head, she started down towards the bottom of the fire escape. Leaping over the railing when several Vetala converged on the bottom of the steps.

Rolling back onto her feet as she landed on the grass, she came up firing at the gathered corpses.

She ignored them falling, breaking into a sprint towards the front of the school.

Chapter Nineteen

Turning towards the door when he heard several gunshots from the other side, Ian raised his P90 and approached the door.

He stopped when someone started banging on the wood.

The girls in the passage all turned towards him.

Stopping by the door, Ian hesitated for a brief moment. "Who are you?"

"It's Cutter, I've got one of the teachers with me. Let us in."

Responding to the voice, Ian unbolted the door and started to pull it open. "We were getting worried about you."

Entering with Jessica behind him, Cutter glanced back as Ian closed the door. "We saw Cat leaving."

Ian nodded, "One of the girls was stabbed. She was injured, she's been unconscious for the last few minutes."

A concerned tone in her voice when she spoke, Jessica looked at Ian. "Where is she?" She watched him indicate one of the dorm rooms and rushed inside. She stopped when she saw Rachel's laid out on the bed, her shirt soaked with her blood. "Oh God."

Ian entered behind her, "Cat's going for one of the vans, she'll bring it here and we'll get her to an hospital."

Following them into the room, Cutter reached the bed and bent down to lift open the shirt. He glanced back at Jessica and Ian after viewing the wound, "Cat needs to hurry."

"It's just up there." Daphne pointed to the trail at the side of the road.

Turning the wheel, Forrest drove up to where the other vans were still parked. Pressing his foot down on the brakes, he climbed out and walked to the fold up chair with the binoculars on it.

He raised them and directed his focus towards the school, "These Vetala, do some of them look like extras from a George Romero movie?"

Taking the binoculars from him, Daphne took her own look at the possessed corpses walking around the school grounds. She almost dropped them when she saw a familiar figure emerge from the main door, "They've killed Amanda and put one of them inside her." She took a few steps back, "What if they've also possessed Catherine and the others as well?"

"You don't need to put a bullet in my head just yet, Daph."

The sound of Catherine's voice made her turn and she rushed forward to kiss her. "I'm glad you're okay."

"One of the girls at the school wasn't so lucky. She's alive but I need to get her to the nearest hospital and quickly." Catherine started towards one of the parked vans, removing the key from the pocket of her jeans.

Slipping out his mobile, Forrest showed it to Catherine. "We can bypass the jamming signal, we can call an ambulance."

Catherine shook her head, "They wouldn't stand a chance with all the Vetala down there."

"Then we'll have to handle it." Forrest slipped the Glock from under his jacket, "But you can't go back down there alone." He glanced back at Daphne, "You'll need both of us for back up."

Sliding open the side door, Catherine climbed into the back of the van. "Ready?"

Nodding, Forrest opened the passenger door and settled onto the seat. "Daph, you're going to have to drive."

Climbing behind the wheel, Daphne watched him lower the window. She looked back at Catherine positioned by the still open side door, twisting the key to start the ignition.

Driving down the trail, Daphne turned onto the road and started towards the school.

Catherine gripped the back of the passenger seat and leaned from the side of the van, aiming her gun as several Vetala came into view.

Shooting down the possessed corpses as the van sped past them, she leaped out onto the gravel as the van started to stop. Rushing towards the side of the school building, she reached the metal steps and began running up to the dorm wing fire exit.

Forrest scrambled from the passenger seat and took up a position at the rear doors, firing at the Vetala that were advancing towards the van.

Lowering the door window, Daphne aimed her Makarov and started shooting.

Chapter Twenty

Jerking his heads towards the fire exit when he heard the banging from the other side, Ian moved when he heard Catherine's voice.

He rushed towards it, glancing back as Cutter emerged from the room where Rachel had been left. "It could be a trick, they tried it before with Amanda."

"Forrest and Daph are here, they're down by the van."

Cutter responded to Catherine's voice, "Get the girl."

Rushing back to the dorm room, Ian lifted Rachel from the bed and gently carried her back towards the fire exit.

Stepping out after Cutter pushed open the thick door, Ian began following Catherine back down to the bottom of the steps.

Catherine made for the front of the van, "Daph, get in the back with Rachel. I'll drive."

Slipping out from behind the wheel, Daphne moved behind Catherine who had begun firing at the Vetala. She stopped when she reached the open side door of the van, turning to watch Ian approach with Rachel in his arms.

Daphne climbed inside the van, turning to help Ian place Rachel on the mattress. "I can take it from here."

Grabbing the handle of the door, Ian slid it shut and moved to the front of the van, looking through the window at Catherine. "Get going."

Stepping out of the way as the van began to reverse, Forrest brought down two more Vetala. He gave the van a quick glance as it started towards the road, turning back to see more possessed corpses begin to file out of the main entrance. "Perhaps we should move this party indoors, too many gatecrashers."

Ian started to run towards the fire escape, firing the P90 at the approaching corpses as he moved.

Keeping up with him, Forrest reached the steps as Ian began going up. Following him up to the dorm fire exit, he rushed passed Cutter moments before he pulled the door shut.

Forrest looked at the girls staring at him, "I suppose you'd all like to get out of here."

Watching him slip out the phone from inside his jacket, Jessica stepped away from the girls under her charge. "That other woman said all the phones were being jammed."

He grinned and started dialling, "This lets me bypass the jamming signal and that lets me call in the cavalry."

Catching sight of the signpost to the hospital at the side of the road, Catherine pressed her foot down hard on the accelerator.

"Almost there."

Her hands covered in Rachel's blood, Daphne did not take her eyes off the girl's motionless face, tears beginning to flow down her cheeks. "Catherine, you can slow down."

Catherine ignored the solemn tone in Daphne's voice, "Just another few minutes and we're there."

Reaching out with her blood covered fingers, Daphne closed the dead girl's eyes. "She's gone."

Pressing her foot down, Catherine brought the van to a halt on the side of the road, slamming the palm of her hand against the wheel.

Chapter Twenty One

Entering through one of the arcade entrances, Forrest descended the stairs and stopped at the beginning of a long passage.

Sitting on a chair outside the mortuary door, Catherine looked down at the tiled floor, her fingers clenched together.

She remained looking down as he reached her, tears dripping from her face. "She would have wanted me to bring her here." Catherine slowly raised her head towards the door opposite her, "Her parents are in there now."

Forrest sat next to her, "You did do everything you could, her death wasn't your vault."

"That blade was meant for me, she saved my life." Catherine looked at him, "What about the other girls, the ones taken over?"

Stroking his beard, he hesitated giving an answer. "A lot of them got away before the assault team even arrived."

The mortuary door opened before he could continue.

Standing up, Catherine focused her tear filled eyes at Rachel's parents. "I am so sorry for your loss."

Opening the door to Alexandra's house, Vladek walked towards the lounge, stopping when he glanced at the open door below the stairs.

Approaching it, he descending into the lit cellar and stopped at the foot of the concrete steps.

Katarina ripped her teeth from the flesh of the dead dog she was kneeling over, her mouth dripping with the animal's blood.

Vladek remained standing silent for a moment, watching her wipe the blood from her chin with the back of her arm. "Put your fangs away, we've got work to do."

Don't miss out!

Visit the website below and you can sign up to receive emails whenever Lee Cushing publishes a new book. There's no charge and no obligation.

https://books2read.com/r/B-A-MYHD-KMSK

BOOKS 2 READ

Connecting independent readers to independent writers.

Also by Lee Cushing

Trust Casefiles
The Trust Casefiles
Pack Hunters
The Girls Of Lakeview Academy
Tourist Trap
The Brides Of Bathory

Standalone
The Other Woman
Heart Of Love, Heart Of Darkness
Demon Vengeance
The Voodoo Mambo
Blood Prey
Her First Time